Author's N

This story is loosely based on the achievements of Sarla Thakral. Sarla was born in 1914. In 1936, she became the first Indian woman to earn her aviation pilot license at the age of twenty-one. She flew the Gypsy Moth solo. After obtaining her initial license, she continued her journey. Sarla completed one thousand hours of flying an aircraft in order to obtain an 'A' license. While she pursued a commercial pilot license in 1939, World War II broke out and civil training was suspended.

Sarla also pursued her other passions. She enjoyed the arts, and went on to train at the Bengal School of Painting and obtained a diploma in Fine Arts.

www.bharatbabies.com

Sarla in the Sky

For more information, please contact:
Mascot Books | 560 Herndon Parkway #120 | Herndon, VA 20170
info@mascotbooks.com

Library of Congress Control Number: 2016910220

CPSIA Code: PRT0816A
ISBN-13: 978-1-63177-746-2

Printed in the United States

Sarla in the Sky

Written by: Anjali Joshi | Art by: Lisa Kurt

Sarla sat at her desk,
Staring at the blue sky.
She saw birds over trees,
Soaring ever so high.

"I wish I was a bird,"
Sarla let out a sigh.
"Don't be silly," said Prem,
"Little girls cannot fly!"

Her friend Prem was right,
Sarla knew it to be true.
Without feathers and wings
She simply could not do.

On very windy days,
She would fly her blue kite.
Sarla tugged on the strings,
As it flew out of sight.

"I wish I was a kite,"
Sarla let out a sigh.
"Don't be silly," said Prem,
"Little girls cannot fly!"

One dewy summer day
Between thick blades of grass,
Sarla lay day-dreaming
Of planes that flew past.

Hanging on a low branch
A small cocoon revealed
The beautiful creature
It had once concealed.

The butterfly fluttered,
Landing on Sarla's nose,
Intently listening
To the little girl's woes.

"I wish I was a butterfly,"
Sarla let out a sigh.
"Then, just like that, I too,
Would be free in the sky."

It was at that moment,
Sarla realized the truth:
The caterpillar must
Have felt the same way too.

"Prem!" Sarla exclaimed,
Too excited to stay cool,
"If a caterpillar can grow wings,
There's nothing I can't do!"

With those five little words,
Her small dream would transform.
One day Sarla would fly,
Of this fact, she was sure.

Prem just nodded his head,
Not knowing what to say.
She was on to something,
That was as clear as day.

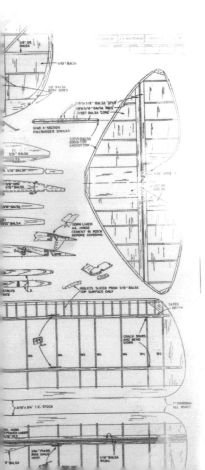

Slowly days turned to weeks
And the months turned to years,
Sarla never lost sight
Of the goal she held dear.

The hurdles were many,
Some people were mean.
They told Sarla that planes
Had no place in her dreams.

"Sarla, planes are for boys,"
The naysayers would say.
To that, calmly she spoke,
"Words won't get in my way."

"There's nothing about wings
That makes them just for a boy.
You should do whatever
Brings you the greatest joy.

What a thrill it would be
To feel wind in my hair,
And soar through giant clouds,
Without the slightest care."

Struck by Sarla's wisdom,
Silence fell on the crowd.
A trailblazer, no doubt,
Sarla would make them proud.

It was no easy task,
But Sarla got it done.
She received her pilot license
At age twenty-one.

A feeling came over her,
One she couldn't describe,
Like a caterpillar
Who had just learned to fly.

Aboard the Gypsy Moth,
In the new pilot seat,
Sarla flew solo
Over buildings and trees.

She spread her wings
Like a beautiful butterfly.
The wind lifted her up,
As she soared through the sky.

Below people gathered,
They stared in awe and gazed.
"Sarla proved them all wrong!"
They exclaimed, simply amazed.

In 1936,
Sarla took her first flight,
The first woman in India
To go to such heights.

When Sarla's plane touched down,
She could not help but beam.
Sarla had fought the odds,
And followed her big dreams.

Sarla's oldest friend, Prem,
Came to watch the big show.
As the months and years passed,
He had watched her dreams grow.

At this moment, her friend
Felt his heart fill with pride.
That small girl who once dreamed
Now had the world on her side.

He stood there, a bit stunned.
He could not believe his eyes.
She'd done it. She'd shown him
Just how high girls can fly.